P9-DXK-782

Zeke Meeks is published by
Picture Window Books
A Capstone Imprint
1710 Roe Crest Drive
North Mankato, MN 56003
www.capstonepub.com

Library of Congress Cataloging-in-Publication Data
Green, D. L. (Debra L.), author.
  Zeke Meeks vs. the pain-in-the-neck pets / by D.L. Green; illustrated by Josh Alves.
      pages cm. — (Zeke Meeks)
  Summary: Zeke wants to bring home the class hamster, so to prove that he is responsible he promises his mother that he will take care of the family dog for a whole week--after that it is one disaster after another.
  ISBN 978-1-4795-2166-1 (hardcover) — ISBN 978-1-4795-3811-9 (paper over board) — ISBN 978-1-4795-5234-4 (ebook)
1. Middle-born children—Juvenile fiction. 2. Hamsters—Juvenile fiction. 3. Pets—Juvenile fiction. 4. Responsibility in children—Juvenile fiction. 5. Elementary schools--Juvenile fiction. [1. Middle-born children—Fiction. 2. Hamsters—Fiction. 3. Pets—Fiction. 4. Responsibility—Fiction. 5. Schools—Fiction. 6. Humorous stories.] I. Alves, Josh, illustrator. II. Title. III. Title: Zeke Meeks versus the pain-in-the-neck pets. IV. Series: Green, D. L. (Debra L.) Zeke Meeks.
  PZ7.G81926Zgu 2014
  813.6—dc23   2013028523

Vector Credits: Shutterstock
Book design: K. Carlson

Printed in the United States of America in Stevens Point, Wisconsin.
092013   007765WZS14

Runaway Waggles!

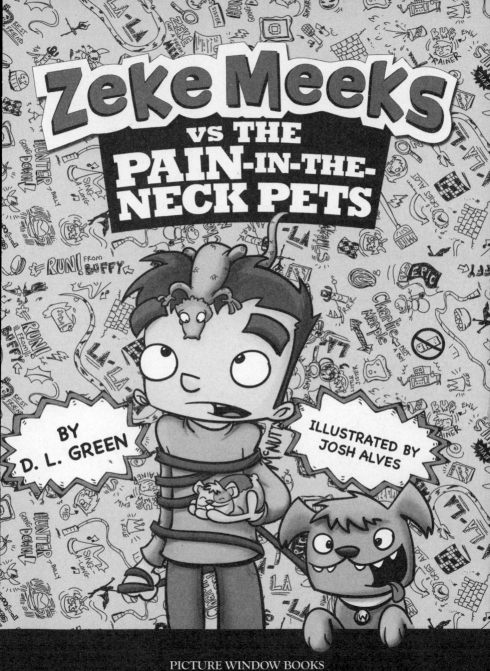

Zeke Meeks
vs THE PAIN-IN-THE-NECK PETS

BY
D. L. GREEN

ILLUSTRATED BY
JOSH ALVES

PICTURE WINDOW BOOKS
a capstone imprint

Inspector Brown Hamster

TABLE OF

Hard to believe,
but true fact.

Waggles and I
learned that
the hard way.
Believe me.

BOYS RULE EVERYTHING BUT THE PLAYGROUND

I don't know which is worse:
Bugs or Grace Chang and her
evil fingernails.

CONTENTS

This is madness.

Yes, it's a day that has something
to do with clocks.

GIRLS DROOL ALL BUT GRACE — SHE BITES

Grace Chang should
come with a warning
sign: BEWARE OF NAILS.

I RULE

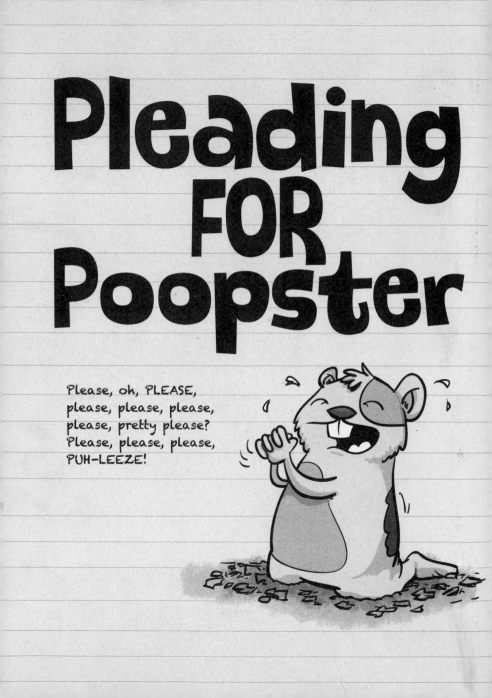

It was Monday, the worst day of the week. It was morning, the worst time of day. It was raining, the worst kind of weather. I was in class, the worst place to be. I was so unhappy.

"Hi, Zeke. I'm so happy," my friend Danny Ford said.

"How can you be happy on a rainy Monday morning at school? Did your brain ooze out of your head?" I asked.

Danny moved his fingers all over his head.

Then he said, "I don't feel any squishiness in my hair or any holes in my head. My brain must be safe inside my head. I'm happy because I'm returning Poopster to the classroom. I took care of him at my house all weekend. It was really hard."

I looked at Poopster, our cute little class hamster. He was sleeping in his cage, as usual. Taking care of him would be easy.

"Poopster was so much trouble. He ruined my weekend," Danny said.

Danny *must* have lost his brain. Maybe he had showered after his brain had oozed out of his head. Then his hair wouldn't be squishy, and his brain would be down the drain.

I would love to bring Poopster home for the weekend. Poopster could sit on my lap while I watched TV and played video games. I could train him to play dead and then jump up and scare people. We'd have so much fun.

I walked over to Mr. McNutty, my teacher, and told him, "I'd like to take Poopster home on Friday."

"Have you cared for a hamster before?" Mr. McNutty asked me.

"Of course," I said. I cared very much for Poopster. I was crazy about him.

"Good." Mr. McNutty handed me a book. "Make sure you read this book about hamsters. And we'll discuss hamster care at lunchtime on Friday."

"Thank you," I said. Though I wasn't happy about spending lunchtime with my teacher instead of my friends.

The morning bell rang. I spent the rest of the day being tortured. I won't torture you with the details. In summary:

- I had to do math problems that would have made Albert Einstein cry.

- I was forced to do a dumb craft project using purple flowers and pink hearts.

- We had a rainy day lunch schedule. That meant staying in the boring classroom and watching a boring movie about boring people in boring places doing boring things.

I finally got home about a million hours later. Waggles jumped all over me. Waggles is our dog. He is the greatest dog ever. He has the worst name ever. He was named by Alexa and Mia, the most annoying sisters ever.

Waggles was wearing a pink ballet tutu. My sisters liked to dress him up in girly stuff. As I said, they are the most annoying sisters ever.

Waggles licked my face a bunch of times. He also drooled on it.

I petted him and said, "Waggles, I can't wait for you to meet Poopster, our class hamster. I'm going to bring him home this weekend. You'll love Poopster. You love everyone — even Mia and Alexa."

Mia and Alexa frowned at me.

My mom said, "Zeke, you can't bring home Pooper."

"Okay, I won't. I'll bring home *Poopster*," I said.

"You can't bring home Poopster."

"Hamsters are great," Mia said. "Princess Sing-Along's best friend is a hamster."

Princess Sing-Along wasn't real. She was an awful character on an awful kiddie TV show that Mia loved and I despised.

Mia started singing a song from the show.

"Who has a furry rear end, la la la. It's my little hamster friend, la la la."

Mom said, "Mia, you can watch Princess Sing-Along's hamster on TV. Zeke, you can play with Poopy the hamster at school. But you can't bring home any hamsters."

"His name is Poopster, not Poopy," I said.

"Well, you can't bring him home. Hamsters are too much work," Mom said.

"It's just for a weekend. I promise to take care of him," I said.

Mom shook her head. "Before we got Waggles, you kids promised to take care of *him*."

"I do take care of him. I often sleep with Waggles, and I pet him a lot," I said.

"And I dress him in pretty bows and skirts and tutus," Mia said.

Mom crossed her arms. "That's just a small part of taking care of a pet. I'm the one who feeds Waggles and keeps him clean and healthy."

I'LL FEED POOPSTER AND KEEP HIM CLEAN AND HEALTHY.

"And I'll help," Mia said.

Mom shook her head again.

"What if I take care of Waggles all week to prove that I can care for an animal? Then will you let me bring Poopster home this weekend?" I asked.

"I don't know," Mom said.

"Please!" I pleaded.

"Fine," Mom said. "But you have to take care of Waggles *all* week."

"I will."

"I'll help," Mia said.

"It will be easy and fun," I said.

"Good." Mom handed me a broom. "Start by sweeping Waggles's dog fur from the floor. Then scoop up his poop from the backyard."

Okay, maybe taking care of Waggles wouldn't be so easy and fun.

The GROSSEST, SECOND Grossest, and

THIRD Grossest Things EVER
(Plus Other Gross Things)

After I swept up the dog fur from the kitchen, Mom gave Mia and me gloves and a bag. She said, "I just scooped Waggles's poop from the yard yesterday. So there won't be much for you to pick up today."

We went in the backyard to look for dog doo. Waggles followed us.

Mia said, "Have you heard Princess Sing-Along's song about backyards?"

I said, "Please don't sing any —"

Before I could finish, Mia sang in a screechy voice: "If you really have to pee, la la la, you can go behind a tree, la la la. But there's one thing you should not do, la la la: Use your backyard for number two, la la la."

"That song is the grossest thing ever," I said.

A large fly zoomed through the air, right toward me.

I held back a scream. Flies scared me. All bugs scared me. I didn't admit that to Mia. I never admitted it to anyone. Instead, I said, "Let's go inside. There's no dog doo in the backyard."

"Yes there is. I know there is," Mia said.

I shook my head. "You don't know that."

"I do too. I just stepped in it." Mia lifted her foot. Under her shoe was a messy mass of squishy, stinky dog doo.

I had been wrong. The Princess Sing-Along song about kids pooping in the backyard was not the grossest thing ever. The messy mass of squishy, stinky dog doo under Mia's shoe was the grossest thing ever.

Mia and I spent the next ten minutes
plugging our noses and cleaning her shoe.

The only thing grosser than a messy mass
of squishy, stinky dog doo on Mia's shoe was a
messy mass of squishy, stinky dog doo on our
plastic gloves.

Suddenly, the fly flew into the poop on my
glove and got stuck in it. The messy mass of
squishy, stinky dog doo with a fly on top was
the grossest thing ever. It was scary too.

Mia and I tossed our gloves into the bag Mom had given us. Then we threw the bag in the trash can outside.

"We're finally done. Let's go inside," I said.

Just then, Waggles crouched down and pooped in the yard.

I sighed, got more gloves, and threw away the new dog doo.

After Mia and I returned to the house, Mom asked, "Did everything go okay?"

"Perfectly," I lied. Lying is always wrong. Except sometimes.

I washed my hands, sat on the couch, and said, "Time for video games."

"Not so fast. Take Waggles for a walk." Mom handed me the leash.

"I'll help," Mia said.

"Only if you promise not to sing Princess Sing-Along songs or step on dog doo," I said.

"Okay," she said.

"Actually, don't step on any doo. No dog logs, bird turd, rat droppings, bat guano, cow pies, beetle dung, or any other kind of poop."

"Okay, I promise," Mia said.

I put on Waggles's leash, which was an embarrassing shade of pink. Then again, all shades of pink are embarrassing. I held the leash as Mia, Waggles, and I left the house.

After we walked about a block, I let Mia hold the leash. It was a nice day. I sped ahead of Mia and Waggles and whistled a happy tune.

Waggles ran up to me. His leash dragged on the ground.

Uh-oh. Mia must have dropped the leash. I reached down to grab it. But Waggles rushed past me.

I screamed, "Waggles! Come back!" But he kept running.

Mia and I chased after him. Mia said, "Zeke, this is your fault. You ran ahead and whistled. Waggles ran to catch up to you."

"It's your fault he got away. You dropped the leash," I said.

I ran and ran. I ran by our neighbor Hunter Down, a very big and very mean kid. He yelled, "Zeke the Freak!"

I ran by our neighbor Mr. Ellis, a very old and very mean man. He yelled, "Get away from my lawn!"

I kept running after Waggles. Then I fell into a large, muddy puddle and got wet and filthy.

Finally, I caught up with Waggles and grabbed his leash. He was wet and filthy too. He must have slipped in the same puddle.

Waggles jumped all over me, making me wetter and filthier.

We walked toward our house. Mia joined us and said, "That was fun."

I shook my head. "I didn't have fun. I got mud all over me."

"It's not all over you. It's just on your shirt and pants and arms and hands and face and neck," she said. "Oh, the mud *is* all over you. Except for a little tiny spot on your left shoulder. I can help get the mud off of you."

"I don't want your help cleaning mud or walking Waggles or scooping his poop or anything else. You only make things worse," I said.

Mia frowned.

We walked the rest of the way in silence.

When we got home, Mom was in her bedroom. She called out, "How was your walk?"

"Perfect. I'm good at taking care of pets," I said. Then I hurried to the bathroom to shower off the mud before Mom could see me.

Do Hamsters SPEAK Gerbil?

Do hamsters speak anything?

At school the next day, I looked into Poopster's cage and whispered, "I'm working hard for you. I had to chase my dog. I fell into a mud puddle. And I had to wipe dog doo from my sister's shoe."

Poopster squeaked.

"Aww. It's okay," I whispered. "I can't wait to take you home."

"Zeke the Freak Meeks, are you really talking to a hamster?" Grace Chang asked.

Grace was short and thin and dressed very girly. Today she wore a pink outfit and a flower in her hair. People who didn't know her thought she seemed sweet.

But people who found out about Grace's hobbies knew she was really evil. Grace's hobbies were:

- Threatening to rip people's faces off.

- Sharpening her long fingernails so she could rip people's faces off.

- Ripping people's faces off.

I didn't personally know anyone who had gotten his or her face ripped off. But I had heard that Grace ripped off a lot of faces. And her long, sharp fingernails looked perfect for face-ripping.

"Zeke the Freak, don't you know that hamsters don't speak English?" Grace said.

"Yeah. Hamsters don't speak English,"
Emma G. said. Emma G. stood behind Grace.

"Yeah. Hamsters don't even speak Spanish
or French," Emma J. said. Emma J. stood behind
Grace too. Both the Emmas always agree with
everything Grace says.

"Do you think hamsters speak Pig Latin?"
Emma G. asked.

"I don't know. I wonder whether they speak dog or snake or dolphin," Emma J. said.

"Be quiet, Emmas. Your silliness is ruining my evilness," Grace said. Then she bent down, put her face next to the hamster cage, and said, "Hi, Poopster-Woopster-Shmoopster. You are *soooo* adorable. I want to kiss you and cuddle with you all day long."

"He doesn't speak English," I said.

She ignored me. She told the hamster, "Oh, my darling little Poopster. I can't wait to take you home this weekend."

"*I'm* taking Poopster home this weekend. Mr. McNutty already told me I could," I said.

Danny Ford walked over. He said, "I never want to take Poopster home again. He was so hard to take care of. He ruined my weekend."

HOW **DARE** YOU TALK ABOUT DARLING LITTLE POOPSTER LIKE THAT!

"Yeah. How dare you!" Emma G. said.

"Yeah. How dare you! Do you think hamsters speak giraffe language?" Emma J. asked.

"I don't know. Do giraffes speak any language?" Emma G. asked.

"Do giraffes and hamsters ever hang out together?" Emma J. asked.

"I told you two Emmas to be quiet. Get out of here," Grace said.

They got out, of course. The Emmas always listen to whatever Grace says.

"Danny, hamsters are easy to take care of," Grace said.

"Yeah. A nice animal like Poopster could never ruin a kid's weekend," I said.

"Are you taking Grace's side on this?" Danny asked me.

I thought about that for a minute. Then I said, "Wow. I guess I am. For the first time ever, Grace and I agree about something." That was really scary.

But not as scary as what happened next.

I need to take a break. Even writing this stuff down is scary.

Okay, I'm back.

I'm warning you. This is really scary. Don't blame me if you get nightmares.

Here goes: Grace swung all ten of her long, sharp, evil fingernails near my face. She said, "Tell Mr. McNutty that you changed your mind. Tell him you don't want to bring Poopster home. I'm taking him this weekend."

"No," I said. My voice was squeakier than the hamster's.

Grace moved her long, sharp, evil fingernails even closer to my face. She said, "If I can't have Poopster, then you can't have a face. I will rip it off of you."

I told you that part was scary.

It's wrong to tell lies. People should never, ever do it. Unless they really want to take home the class pet and really, really don't want their faces ripped off.

I told Grace, "You should wait until next weekend to bring Poopster home. You'll get more time with him because we don't have school next Monday."

"We don't?" she asked.

"We don't?" Danny asked.

We did. I had lied because I didn't want my face ripped off. I liked my face.

I didn't love my thick eyebrows or my wide mouth or my square forehead. But I still liked them better *on* me than ripped *off* me.

So I told Grace, "There's a new holiday next Monday called . . ."

I stopped talking and tried to make up a holiday. I looked around the classroom for ideas. I also looked for a shield to guard my face against Grace's nails.

Finally, I saw the clock on the wall and said, "Clock Day. The new holiday next Monday is Clock Day, to honor the person who invented the clock."

"Who invented the clock?" Danny asked.

"That's not important," I said.

"If we're having an entire holiday to honor that person, then it's important," Grace said.

"Okay. It's . . . um . . . It's Mrs. Clock, of course."

"What's her full name?" Danny asked.

I looked around the room again. "Chair. Marker. Clock. I mean, her name is Cheryl Martha Clock. She invented the perfect way to show the time."

"Inventing a clock seems easy," Grace said.

"Sharon Marla Clock made it look easier than it really was."

"I thought her name was Cheryl Martha Clock," Grace said.

"Oh, yeah. Anyway, you know the big hand and the little hand on the clock?" I asked.

"I don't know them personally," Grace said.

"But you know *of* them."

"Yeah. I know about the big hand and the little hand," Grace said.

"In Mrs. Clock's first try at inventing the clock, the big hand and little hand were *feet*."

"What are you talking about?" Victoria Crow asked as she walked over to us.

Victoria Crow was the smartest kid in third grade. She was smart enough to know that there were no holidays about clocks. And she probably knew the real name of the person who had invented the clock.

If Victoria told Grace that I had been fooling her about Clock Day, I'd have to say goodbye to my face. Grace would rip it right off me.

I said, "Grace, you should hurry to tell Mr. McNutty that you want to take home Poopster next weekend."

"Good idea." She left.

Phew.

I put my face near Poopster's and began whispering to him.

"You'll have much more fun at my house than at Grace's house," I whispered. "I have good video games and normal fingernails. Plus, I'm not evil. In fact, I'm pretty nice, even though I lied. We'll have a great time this weekend."

I sure hoped so. It would be my last weekend before Grace found out I was lying about Clock Day and ripped my face off.

When I got home from school, Mom said, "Don't forget to take Waggles for a walk today. And give him a bath. For some reason, he's covered in mud."

I knew the reason: yesterday's mud puddle.

"Do you know how Waggles got muddy?" Mom asked.

It is wrong to lie. If I told Mom I didn't know how Waggles got mud all over him, that would be a lie. So I didn't tell Mom that. I didn't tell her anything.

Instead, I said, "Come on, Waggles. It's bath time."

My sister Mia said, "You should give Waggles a bath *after* his walk. I'll help you."

"No. I'll do it my way. And I don't need your help. Giving a dog a bath is easy," I said, though I'd never given a dog a bath before.

I plugged the bathtub drain, turned on the faucet, and started filling the tub with warm water. Then I put an old towel and dog shampoo next to the tub. Easy as pie. (Well, it was easy as *eating* pie. It wasn't as easy as *making* pie. I don't know how to make pie.)

I went to get Waggles.

I couldn't find him.

I called out his name. I whistled. I looked around the house. I still couldn't find him. Okay, this wasn't so easy.

Finally, I spotted Waggles under my bed.
I lay on my rug and reached for him. Just as I
was about to grab him, he ran away.

I chased him all over the house until I
couldn't run any further.

I took a break. I went to the kitchen and ate
a yummy peanut butter cookie.

That gave me a great idea. I grabbed a bunch of cookies. Then I held one out and called for Waggles.

Once he came near the kitchen, I waved the cookie and started walking toward the bathroom.

Waggles followed me. Actually, he followed the cookie.

Mia followed Waggles. She sang a Princess Sing-Along song: "Listen to Mr. Vet, la la la. Don't feed sweets to your pet, la la la."

"What's wrong with sweets? Waggles loves sweets," I said.

She sang, "After your pet's sweets are chewed, la la la, they may end up puked and spewed, la la la."

"*Eww.* Well, tempting Waggles with cookies is the only way I can get him into the bathtub," I said.

"I can help get Waggles in the tub," Mia said.

I shook my head. "I told you I don't need your help."

I got to the bathroom. Uh-oh. I'd left the water running in the bathtub. While I was chasing Waggles and eating a snack, water had filled the tub and spilled onto the bathroom floor.

I shut off the faucet, drained some of the water, put towels on the floor, and threw the cookie into the tub.

Waggles jumped in. As he ate a bunch of cookies, I shampooed, rinsed, and dried him.

I had to dry myself too. I'd gotten soaking wet. And I was exhausted. I ate the last cookie I'd taken.

Finally, I plopped onto the couch to play a video game. That's when Mom said, "Take Waggles for a walk before it gets dark."

I sighed and got the leash.

Mia said, "I can get you an umbrel—"

"I don't want your help," I said.

I led Waggles outside. He looked nice and clean. I gripped the leash tightly so he couldn't run off again.

I didn't need my little sister's help. Waggles and I were doing great.

Then it started raining. I wished someone had told me to take an umbrella.

Waggles and I ran for the house to get out of the rain. I tripped on Waggles's leash and fell into a mud puddle. Waggles jumped in after me and rolled in the mud.

When we got home, Mom said, "You and Waggles are full of mud. You both need baths. And brush Waggles's fur afterward."

I wished I'd waited until after the walk to give Waggles his bath.

I fed Waggles cookies while I bathed him again. Then I gave Waggles more cookies so he'd sit still while I brushed his fur. Finally, I got out a video game and sat on the couch.

Mom told me I had to do my homework first.

After my homework, it was time for dinner.

Finally, I turned on my video game.

"What happened to all the cookies I made for the school bake sale?" Mom asked.

Oops. It is wrong to tell a lie. So I didn't answer her.

Mia said, "Zeke ate one cookie and gave Waggles the rest."

"That's a lie," I said. "I ate *two* cookies and gave Waggles the rest."

Mom sent me to my room.

A few minutes later, she yelled, "Get out here, Ezekiel Heathcliff Meeks!"

She called me by my full name only when she was really mad. Also, she yelled only when she was really mad. Since she had called me by my full name *and* yelled, she must have been really, *really* mad.

I didn't know why Mom wanted me out of my bedroom. But I was pretty sure it wasn't to give me a giant candy bar or a new video game or even a big hug. I slowly opened my door and walked out of my room.

There Really Is Such a Thing as

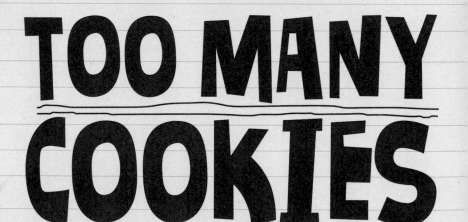

Please don't barf, please don't barf, please don't barf...

TOO MANY COOKIES

Grossest. Day. Of. My. LIFE. Read at your own risk.

"Watch out!" Mia said as I walked out of my bedroom.

"Stop telling me what to do. I don't need your help," I said. Then I stepped in something gooey.

I looked down. Yuck. My foot was wading in a slimy and chunky mound of dog barf. I said, "That is the grossest, stinkiest thing I've ever seen."

"Then look at that," she said.

Mia pointed to a bigger mound of dog barf near my foot. Beyond that lay a pile of dog diarrhea that was even grosser and stinkier than the dog barf. Mia said, "I told you that cookies would make Waggles sick."

Mom sighed. "Zeke, you have a lot of cleaning to do. First, clean your foot. After that, clean the hallway."

"Okay," I said.

"And the kitchen," she added.

I sighed. "Waggles barfed in there too?"

"Barfed and pooped," Mia said.

My sister Alexa came out of her bedroom and said, "You need to clean my room too. Waggles barfed on my favorite scarf and pooped in my new shoes."

"It's really gross in there," Mia said.

"Can you help me clean, Mia?" I asked.

She shook her head. "You told me you didn't want my help."

"I changed my mind. I do want your help."

"I changed my mind too. I don't want to help you," she said.

I went over to Waggles, who was lying on the floor and looking weak and sad. I patted his head and said, "Sorry for making you sick."

Then I took out the cleaning supplies and got to work. I spent about a million hours cleaning the barf and poop. Then I washed my hands with about a million gallons of soap and water for about a million minutes.

Then it was time for bed. What a horrible day. I sure hoped a weekend with Poopster would be worth all my suffering.

On Friday, I was so excited about taking
Poopster home that I ignored my teacher even
more than usual. I even stayed in the classroom
during recess so I could visit Poopster. He was
sleeping.

Suddenly, something very sharp pressed
against my back. I had a terrible feeling that I
knew what it was.

I looked behind me. I had been right. Grace
Chang held one of her very sharp fingernails
against my back.

She said, "You'd better take good care of Poopster this weekend."

"I will," I said.

Grace kept her fingernail on my back. She said, "Poopster had better be clean and healthy when I get him next weekend. I have big plans for him. I'm going to show him around my huge bedroom. I'll paint his nails the same color as mine. And we'll celebrate Clock Day. By the way, what do people do on Clock Day?"

It is wrong to lie, unless the person you're lying to is evil and has her very sharp fingernail pressed against your back. Then it's okay. I told Grace, "On Clock Day, people paint clocks on their faces and watch the big Clock Day parade."

My best friend, Hector Cruz, ran into the classroom and rushed over to me. He asked, "What's wrong, Zeke? Should I call a doctor or an ambulance?"

"Nothing's wrong, except for Grace's long, sharp fingernails. They're very wrong. Why? What do you *think* is wrong?" I asked.

"You stayed inside during recess. You never, ever do that," Hector said.

I shrugged. "I just wanted to visit Poopster."

"Hector, what are you doing for Clock Day?" Grace asked.

"Clock Day? What's that?" he asked.

Oh, no. If Grace found out I was lying about Clock Day, she would plunge her sharp, evil fingernail much deeper into my back. Maybe it would even get stuck there, and I'd be attached to Grace all day. She'd probably rip my face off. So I said, "Hector, how could you forget about Clock Day?"

"Clock Day? Huh?" He scratched his head.

I pointed to Poopster, who was still sleeping. I said, "Did you hear that? Poopster just squeaked something that sounded like 'Grace.' I think he's trying to talk to you, Grace."

Grace bent over the cage and said, "My darling, loveable, wuvable Poopster. You know my name!"

While she did that, I whispered to Hector, "Pretend that Clock Day is a real holiday."

Hector nodded. Then he said loudly, "I can't wait for Clock Day. I'm going to buy a new clock."

"Only one? I'm going to buy *three* new clocks," Grace said. "By the way, I just heard Poopster squeak again. His squeak sounded like 'I love Grace.'"

"You told me Poopster didn't speak English," I said.

Grace dug her nail into my back again.

Luckily, the bell rang and we returned to our desks.

I let out a big breath. *Phew.* Grace still believed my dumb lie about Clock Day. But I should have invented a better holiday. I should have told her it was Zeke Meeks Day, a day on which everyone gave me money.

I looked at the classroom clock. In four more hours, school would end and I could bring Poopster home. I wondered why time passed so slowly in class and so quickly at recess and lunchtime. If I had known who really invented the clock, I would have asked her about that.

At lunchtime, I had to stay in the classroom so Mr. McNutty could tell me about hamsters. He said, "Hamsters need to be handled gently. They're small animals."

Duh. Of course they're small animals.

I peered into the cage. Poopster was tiny. He was sleeping. He looked like a cute little ball of fur. I wondered if he snored. I pressed my ear against the cage.

"Zeke, are you paying attention?" Mr. McNutty asked. "I'm trying to teach you about hamsters."

I nodded. I was paying attention to Poopster. That was a great way to learn about hamsters. I had just learned that he snored.

"Did you read the hamster book?" Mr. McNutty asked.

I nodded again. I'd forgotten all about the book Mr. McNutty had given me. But I probably had read a book with a hamster in it sometime in my life.

"As the book explained, hamsters are nocturnal," my teacher said.

I nodded again.

I didn't know what nocturnal meant. But I could read about it when I took the book home this weekend. It was probably somewhere in my desk.

While Mr. McNutty talked about hamsters, I ignored him and ate my lunch. I didn't need Mr. McNutty's help. Taking care of Poopster would be easy. And the book would explain anything I didn't know.

I heard balls bouncing outside. My friends were probably on the playground. I hoped Hector would save a cookie for me. I saved some chips for him.

"And, Zeke, a few more things," my teacher said.

I looked at him. While Mr. McNutty talked about hamsters, I thought about his hair. His hairpiece seemed a little crooked today.

I wondered what he used to stick it on his head. Whatever it was, it didn't work very well. His hairpiece had fallen off a few times this year. He was totally bald.

"So that's it, Zeke. Any questions?" Mr. McNutty asked.

"Yes. Do you miss having real hair?" I asked.

He frowned. "Do you have any questions about hamsters?"

"Yes. Do all hamsters snore like Poopster?"

"I don't know. Any other questions?"

I nodded. "Does your hairpiece make your head itchy? Also, why does time move so much slower in class than anywhere else?"

He sighed and said, "Zeke, go on the playground for the rest of lunchtime. I need a few minutes of peace."

"If you let me stay on the playground for an hour, you can have an hour of peace," I said.

"That would be great. But no. Goodbye," he said.

I waved goodbye to Mr. McNutty and Poopster. Then I ran out to the playground.

When I got home from school, I shouted, "He's here! He's finally here! Here's Poopster, the best animal in the whole world!"

Waggles barked.

"Waggles thinks *he's* the best animal in the whole world," Mia said.

I set Poopster's cage on the kitchen table. Then I patted my dog. "Sorry, Waggles. You're just not as cute as Poopster. And you're a lot harder to take care of. You drool and throw up and have big, stinky poops."

My sister Alexa glanced up from the computer and said, "Keep it down. I'm trying to do my homework."

"No she's not. She's looking at pictures of rock stars' tattoos," Mia said.

"Tattletale," Alexa said.

"Does Poopster need anything from the pet store?" Mom asked.

I opened my backpack and took out Poopster's food, food bowl, water bottle, treats, chew toys, exercise wheel, running tube, litter pan, nesting paper, jungle gym, and igloo hideout. "Well, I don't know. Do you think he has enough stuff?" I asked.

"More than enough," Mom said.

Then I realized I'd left the hamster book at school. Oh, well. I didn't need any help.

I looked into Poopster's cage and asked, "Are you ready to play?" But Poopster was sleeping.

I stared at him for a long time. Poopster kept sleeping.

I ate a snack. Poopster kept sleeping.

I did my homework. Poopster kept sleeping.

I brought his cage outside while I played with my neighbor. Poopster kept sleeping.

I took Poopster into the house and watched TV. Poopster kept sleeping.

My family ate dinner. Poopster kept sleeping.

Mia said, "Zeke, you told me Poopster was fun. All he does is sleep."

"As soon as he wakes up, we'll play with him. It'll be a lot of fun," I said.

But Poopster kept sleeping. He slept while I played video games, changed into my pajamas, carried his cage into my bedroom, turned off the light, and fell asleep.

I had a great dream. I was hanging out with professional basketball players. We played basketball and video games and ate chocolate-marshmallow-cherry cupcakes. I had just performed an awesome slam dunk when a screeching noise woke me.

I sat up in bed, clutched my blanket against my chest, and shook. The sounds of *screech, screech, screech, screech, screech* filled my bedroom. Something awful was in my room. Maybe it was a monster or a ghost. Even worse, it might be a bug or Grace Chang.

I slowly and quietly reached for my flashlight under my bed. I shined it in the direction of the awful screeching noise.

Oh. It was Poopster, running on his exercise wheel. "Poopster, you ruined my great dream. Go to sleep," I said.

But Poopster kept running on his wheel. *Screech, screech, screech, screech, screech.*

I probably should have listened to Danny Ford when he said Poopster wasn't easy to take care of.

I put my pillow over my head to keep out the noise. But Poopster's loud screeches came through loud and clear.

It took a long time to fall back to sleep. And I didn't return to my great dream. Instead, I had nightmares about disgusting dog barf, Grace's sharp, evil nails, and a horrible, screeching clock.

On Saturday morning, Poopster was still running on his wheel, screeching louder than ever. Oh, well. Now that we were both awake, I could finally play with him.

My mom walked into my room and said, "The bathtub is full of dog fur and mud. You need to clean it."

"I will, after I play with Poopster," I said.

"Now," she said.

Ugh. It took me a long, disgusting time to clean the tub.

By the time I returned to my room, Poopster was asleep again. This was ridiculous. I decided that since he had woken me last night, I could wake him this morning. I opened his cage and put my hand in to pick him up.

Poopster bit me!

"Ow!" I screamed, even though it was just a little nip on the tip of my finger. I yanked my hand out of the cage and closed the door.

Mia walked into my room. She asked, "Did Poopster bite you?"

"None of your business," I said.

"I can help you," she said.

"I don't need any h—" I was about to say I didn't need any help. Then I realized I needed a lot of help. So I asked Mia, "How can you help me?"

"I can sing Princess Sing-Along songs."

I shook my head. "That is not helping. That is the opposite of helping. That is harming."

Mia sang a Princess Sing-Along song anyway: "Hamsters stay up at night, la la la. And a few of them bite, la la la. Something else I've been taught, la la la. Hamsters can poop a lot, la la la."

That song was annoying, but it was true. Poopster stayed awake at night. He had just bitten me. I looked in Poopster's cage. He had pooped a lot. There was a good reason he was called Poopster.

"Poopster is like Silky Sadie," Mia said.

"Huh?" I asked.

"Princess Sing-Along got Silky Sadie for Christmas. She's a hamster. I mean Silky Sadie is a hamster, not Princess Sing-Along. Princess Sing-Along and her brother, Prince Dance-Along, take care of Silky Sadie. Silky Sadie is Princess Sing-Along's best Christmas present ever."

I don't think she even took a breath . . . and she was still talking:

"Princess Sing-Along also has a doll named Tiny Tatiana. She wants a cat for her birthday. She'll name it Caterina if it's a girl, and either Evan or Jon-Paul Jonathan if it's a boy. And she —"

"Stop," I said. "I thought you were going to help me with Poopster."

"You asked about Silky Sadie. So I was telling you about her and Prince Dance-Along and Tiny Tatiana and —"

"Stop!" I screamed.

Mia frowned. "You're rude."

"Please just tell me what you learned about the hamster, Silly Sofie," I said.

"There's no hamster named Silly Sofie," Mia said.

I sighed. "You just told me that Princess Sing-Along got a hamster for her birthday."

"Princess Sing-Along never got a hamster for her birthday."

I was getting a headache. I begged Mia, "Please just tell me how you know so much about hamsters."

"Because of Princess Sing-Along's hamster. You called her Silly Sofie." Mia shook her head. "That's wrong. Her name is Silky Sadie. Princess Sing-Along got her for Christmas. You said it was for her birthday. That's wrong too. I know it because of this song." Mia sang, "Guess what I got from Santa Claus, la la la. It's furry and it has four paws, la la la. If you guessed dollhouse you are wrong, la la la. Now I will sing another song, la la la."

"No! Please! No! No more songs!" I pressed my hands over my ears.

Then I asked, "Will you help me with Poopster? I don't want him to bite me again."

"Okay," Mia said. "Some hamsters bite if they're surprised. So don't shove your hand in Poopster's cage. Put your hand in slowly instead."

"Thanks. Now can you tell me how to keep Poopster quiet at night so I can sleep?" I asked.

"Hamsters can't help being noisy at night. They stay up at night and sleep during the day. Princess Sing-Along takes Silky Sadie's cage out of her bedroom every night. You should take Poopster's cage out of your room at night too."

I patted Mia's head. "You're little, but you're smart."

She smiled. "Thanks. I'm like a hamster that way."

"Thank you for your help. Now will you help me clean the poop from Poopster's cage?" I asked.

"No way," she said.

I sighed. Then I peered into the cage and told Poopster, "I like you, but you sure are a pain in the neck."

After I learned how to take care of Poopster, I had fun with him. He stayed awake for a few hours every day. I gently held his soft, furry body with two hands and clasped him against my chest. That way, he wouldn't get loose. I fed him treats of carrots and corn. At night, I put his cage in the bathroom so I could sleep.

I was still kind of glad to return him to school on Monday morning. Poopster had pooped all weekend long, like a poop machine set at high speed. He might have set world records for pooping. The only thing worse than smelling Poopster's cage was cleaning it.

As I set his cage on the classroom table, Danny walked up to me. He asked, "How was your weekend?"

"I should have listened to you. Taking care of Poopster was hard," I said.

"I won't be rude and say I told you so," Danny said.

"Thanks."

"Never mind. I can't help myself. Told you so, told you so, told you so," Danny chanted.

"I still had fun with Poopster. And, luckily, I learned about hamster care from an expert," I said.

"What expert? A veterinarian?" Danny asked.

I shook my head.

"A zookeeper?" he asked.

I shook my head again.

"A pet store owner?"

I shook my head again and said, "It's not important who the hamster expert was. But she really knew her stuff." It would be too embarrassing to admit that the expert was my little sister.

And I sure wouldn't admit that my little sister had learned about hamsters from a very annoying singing princess on a kiddie TV show.

My friend Rudy Morse walked over. He said, "Hi, Zeke. Now that you've had Poopster all weekend, you must be good at taking care of pets. Will you take care of my pet when I go on vacation? He's cute, sweet, little, and very easy."

"Sure. I'll take care of him," I said.

"Thanks. You'll love spending next weekend with Cuddles, my giant red beetle."

Giant red beetle? No, no, no, no. And a thousand more times no. Make that a million times no. My voice shook as I said, "I . . . I . . . I'm going on vacation too. Sorry. I can't take care of your giant red beetle."

"Are you going away for Clock Day?" Rudy asked.

"Clock Day?"

"Grace Chang told me about it."

Grace walked over when she heard her name. She said, "Hi, Zeke the Freak. Too bad you only had two and a half days with Poopster. I'll get *three* and a half days with him. *Bah-ha-ha-ha.*" *Bah-ha-ha-ha* was her evil laugh.

"Yeah. *Bah-ha-ha-ha*," Emma G. said. She stood behind Grace.

"Yeah. What they said. *Bah-ha-ha-ha*," Emma J. said. She stood behind Emma G.

Lying is wrong. But sometimes it's okay to lie to evil people. So I told Grace, "You're lucky you get to spend Clock Day with Poopster." Then I silently laughed my own *bah-ha-ha-ha* evil laugh and told a few more lies. "Poopster hardly pooped at all last weekend. He was very easy to take care of. I loved having his cage near my pillow every night."

"I'll put his cage super close to my pillow," Grace said.

"Yeah. Super close," Emma G. said.

"Yeah. Super close," Emma J. said.

"Yeah. Super close," I said.

I hoped Poopster would spend all night loudly running on his hamster wheel, right next to Grace.

I looked at him. He did what he did best: he pooped.

I whispered, "Make sure you poop a lot at Grace's house," and walked away.

NO, NO, NO, NO, NO!

AND SO ON.

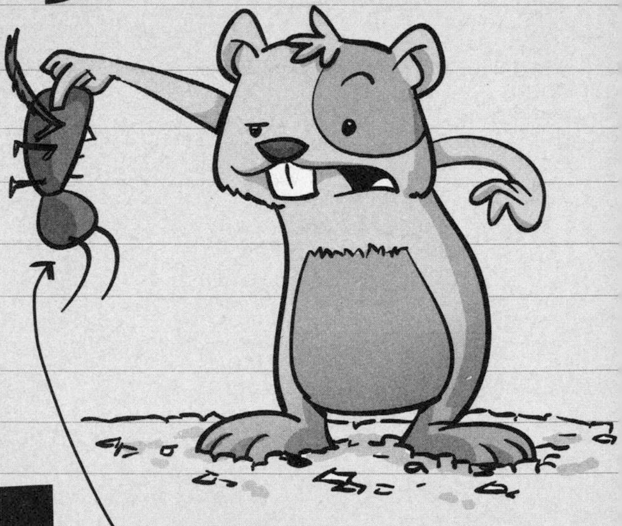

By the time I got home from school, I already missed Poopster.

At least I had Waggles. I gave him extra attention. I played fetch with him, took him for a walk, brushed his fur, and gave him a dog biscuit. I did not feed him any people food. I did not want to clean up any more dog barf or doggy diarrhea.

My big sister, Alexa, walked into our house with her friend Sarah. Alexa was holding a huge lizard.

She said, "Isn't this animal darling!"

It did not look the least bit darling. To tell you the truth, it looked ugly. It had bulging eyes and scaly skin and spikes all over its head and body.

"Do you like my bearded dragon lizard?" Sarah asked.

I shrugged. I didn't like beards or dragons or lizards. I *really* didn't like those things combined in one ugly animal.

"Her name is Lovely Lisa. She's a real sweetheart," Sarah said.

Lisa the lizard didn't look lovely. She also didn't look like a real sweetheart or even a fake sweetheart or any other kind of sweetheart. She looked like a real beast.

Alexa moved closer to me. She was still holding the lizard.

I took a step back.

Alexa said, "You should hold Lovely Lisa. She loves to be held."

"She might love to be held, but I don't love holding lizards. I don't even *like* holding lizards," I said.

"You've never tried holding a lizard. Once you do, you might love it." Alexa moved even closer to me.

I backed farther away, until I was trapped against a wall.

Alexa held her arms out, thrusting the lizard's pointy face next to mine. She said, "Isn't my Lovely Lisa a snuggly-wuggly sweetums?"

I wouldn't call a bearded dragon lizard a snuggly-wuggly sweetums. I wouldn't call anything a snuggly-wuggly sweetums.

Lovely Lisa opened her mouth. She looked like she was smiling.

She looked kind of snuggly and sweet.

"Are you sure you don't want to hold Lovely Lisa?" Sarah asked me.

"I'll try," I said.

Sarah showed me how to hold the lizard. Soon, Lovely Lisa sat in my hands, nice and calm. She moved a lot slower than Poopster did. She didn't wriggle around.

"Bearded dragon lizards are such great pets," Sarah said.

"Is Lovely Lisa noisy at night?" I asked.

"Not at all. I keep her in my bedroom and she never wakes me up."

"Does she poop a lot?" I asked.

"Not really," Sarah said.

"I want a dragon bearded lizard for a pet,"
I said.

Sarah laughed. "You mean bearded dragon lizard."

I nodded.

"She's easy to take care of. She only eats once or twice a day. Do you want to feed Lovely Lisa?" she asked.

"Thanks. I'd love to feed her," I said.

"I left her food on your porch. I'll be right back." Sarah went out the front door.

A minute later, she returned with a big box. A loud chirping sound came from inside the box. Sarah said, "Open the lid a little. Then put Lovely Lisa in the box so she can eat what's inside."

"What's inside the box?" I asked.

"Lovely Lisa's dinner. A cricket, of course," Sarah said. "Bearded dragon lizards love to eat crickets."

"Take Lovely Lisa." I handed her to Sarah. Then I started running.

"Where are you going?" Sarah shouted.

"I just remembered something I need to do," I said as I ran.

The thing I needed to do was to escape from the cricket and the cricket-eating lizard as fast as I could.

"We can wait until you get back so you can feed Lovely Lisa," Sarah said.

"No! No, no, no!" I shouted.

I kept shouting, "No, no, no, no, no!" as I ran out of my house and down the block.

A week later, I lay in bed for a long time. I did not get up when my alarm went off or when my mom shouted, "Wake up!" or when Waggles jumped on my chest. I did not want to go to school. I never wanted to go to school. But this morning I didn't want to go to school even more than usual.

I had told Grace that today was Clock Day. She must have found out by now that Clock Day wasn't real. She probably wanted to rip my face off.

My face belonged on me. It was the perfect size for my head. I wanted to keep it there. It didn't belong on the ground or in Grace's closet or wherever Grace kept the faces that she ripped off.

To save my face, I needed to stay far away from Grace. I'd have to skip school and not come back until she calmed down, probably in about eight to ten years.

I patted Waggles, who was still sitting on my chest. I asked him, "Will you still like me with a ripped-off face?"

Waggles drooled on me.

"I guess that's a yes." I patted him again. "You won't be able to drool on my face once it's ripped off. Unless Grace lets me take home my ripped-off face. I could keep it in my bedroom and let you drool on it every morning. That's how much I love you, Waggles."

Waggles brought over one of his toys. It used to be Alexa's doll, Bella the Beautiful. Waggles had drooled all over it, bitten holes in it, and taken out its stuffing. It no longer looked beautiful, but it was a fun dog toy.

I threw Bella the Beautiful across my room and yelled, "Go fetch!"

Waggles jumped off my bed and ran to get it.

My mom opened my bedroom door and put her hands on her hips. "Ezekiel Heathcliff Meeks, why are you still in bed on a school day? You don't have time to play with Waggles. Get dressed, brush your teeth, and eat breakfast."

I plopped my head on my pillow and said in a fake weak voice, "I'm sick."

Mom walked over to me and felt my forehead. "You aren't warm. And I just saw you playing with Waggles. Don't pretend you're sick."

I sighed and started getting ready for school. After I brushed my teeth, I stared at my face in the bathroom mirror and wondered if I'd ever see it on my head again. I whispered, "Goodbye, poor, sweet face. You've done a good job all these years. You've grown at the same rate as my head."

I signed and then continued, "You've smiled and frowned well. You made great weird expressions to scare my sister Mia. I'll miss you every —"

"Hurry up, Zeke!" my mom yelled.

I waved goodbye to my face and rushed out of the bathroom.

I arrived at school on time with Mom's help. And by "help," I mean she yelled, "Hurry up, Zeke!" all morning.

Before I got out of the car, I put a ski mask over my head. If Grace couldn't see my face, maybe she wouldn't rip it off. Also, I hoped the mask could protect my face from Grace's long, sharp, evil fingernails.

"It's nice out today. Why are you wearing a ski mask over your head?" Mom asked me.

"What? Did you say something about ski wax over my bed? This mask over my face makes it hard to hear," I said. Then I rushed out of the car and closed the door behind me.

I didn't see Grace outside. Maybe she still thought it was Clock Day and was staying home from school. Maybe Poopster had kept her awake all weekend, so she was catching up on her sleep. My best hope was that Grace had moved away — far away, to Australia or the North Pole or, best of all, outer space.

Suddenly, Grace ran over to me, grabbed my ski mask, and pulled it off. She said, "I thought that was you, Zeke the Freak Meeks."

"Yeah. She thought that was you, Zeke the Meeks or something like that," Emma G. said.

"Yeah. She thought that was you, Freak the Zeke or something like that," Emma J. said.

I waved. "Hi, Grace. Hi, Emma G. and Emma J."

"Do you know how I recognized you under the ski mask?" Grace asked.

"Because you saw me get out of my mom's car? Or because —"

"No," Grace interrupted. "It's because only a fool like you would wear a ski mask in nice weather."

"Yeah. What she said. Something about a fool and a ski mask," Emma G. said.

"Yeah. And also nice weather or something," Emma J. said.

Grace pointed at me. Her long, sharp, evil fingernail dangled near my face. She said, "Zeke Meeks, you're a fool for believing in Clock Day. You're also a fool for sleeping in the same room as Poopster. And you're a fool for cleaning Poopster's cage yourself instead of making your parents do it. So when I saw someone foolish enough to wear a ski mask on a nice day, I knew it had to be you."

I grinned, which probably made me look like an even bigger fool. But I didn't care. I was happy that Grace thought I believed in Clock Day. If she had found out I'd lied to her about Clock Day on purpose, I would not have had a face to grin with. *Phew.*

I gave my face a gentle, loving pat. When I got into the classroom, I walked over to Poopster's cage. I looked inside and grinned some more.

Poopster seemed to be grinning back at me.

ABOUT THE AUTHOR

D. L. Green lives in California with her husband, three children, silly dog, and a big collection of rubber chickens. She loves to read, write, and joke around.

ABOUT THE ILLUSTRATOR

Josh Alves took care of a variety of pets as child (including pigeons and rabbits with his grandfather). Today, Josh gets to draw in his studio in Maine where he lives with his amazing wife, four incredible children, and their pet husky.

WHY DON'T SCHOOLS EVER HAVE HORSES FOR CLASS PETS?

(And other really important questions)

Write answers to these questions, or discuss them with your friends and classmates.

1. Why don't schools ever have horses for class pets? Or cats? Or potbellied pigs? What kind of animal would you like for a class pet?

2. Maybe I could have prepared more for Poopster's visit. What would you have done differently?

3. Never in a million years would I have guessed that my little annoying sister could teach me anything. Have you ever learned something from someone younger than you? How did you deal with the embarrassment?

4. What is the best part about having a pet? What is the worst? (It has to be doggy diarrhea, right?)

BIG WORDS
according to Zeke

TRY USING THEM IN SENTENCES JUST LIKE I DO

ADORABLE: A word that girls use to describe things that they think are super cute. But adorable things are actually usually annoying and somewhat gross.

BULGING: Sticking out in a way that might be a little gross or creepy.

CHANTED: Said the same thing over and over and over and over. Chanting is pretty annoying, unless you are the one doing it — then it is fun.

DESPISED: If you hated something more than anything you have ever, ever, ever hated before, then you actually despised it.

DIARRHEA: When a dog has diarrhea, his poop is brown and watery. It is SO gross! EW, EW, EW!

DISGUSTING: Things that make you go "EW!" like love notes, most girls, and diarrhea.

EXHAUSTED: Felt so tired that you are basically a walking zombie.

NOCTURNAL: According to Princess Candy, nocturnal means awake during the night. I found out the hard way that hamsters are nocturnal.

A cat in a princess hat is
ridiculous. But my sisters
would say it's adorable.

PROFESSIONAL: Getting paid for playing a sport. How awesome would that be!?

RIDICULOUS: Very silly and just not right, like Waggles in girly clothes.

SCREECHY: Loud and high-pitched and awful! In other words, everything that has to do with Princess Sing-Along.

SNUGGLY-WUGGLY SWEETUMS: I'm not sure what this means, because it is something that only a girl would say.

SQUEAKY: A sound that is super high and shrill, sure to annoy anyone who hears it.

SQUISHINESS: Mushy and sort of wet, like how your brains would feel if they oozed out of your head.

TATTLETALE: Someone who tells on you for doing something wrong. Boo on tattletales!

THREATENING: Saying you will do something bad to someone. Grace Chang is an expert at threatening. Not a day goes by when she doesn't threaten someone.

TORTURED: Hurt someone in a terrible, awful, horrible way. Torture is another one of Grace Chang's expert topics.

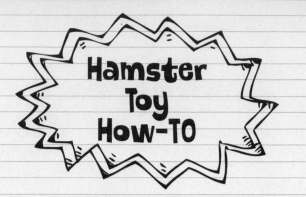

Hamster Toy How-To

Once I started learning about hamsters, I didn't want to stop. I found out that hamsters have to chew on things to keep their teeth short and healthy. They also need to play and feel challenged, or they won't be happy. Things that might seem like garbage to some people make pretty great toys for Poopster and his pals.

Here are some ways you can make your own toys:

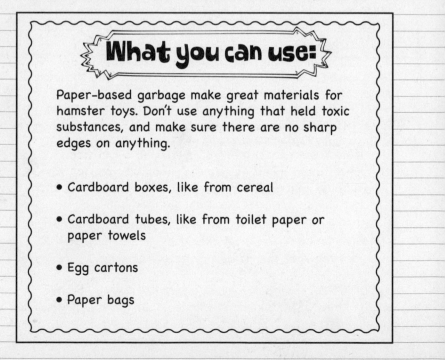

What you can use:

Paper-based garbage make great materials for hamster toys. Don't use anything that held toxic substances, and make sure there are no sharp edges on anything.

- Cardboard boxes, like from cereal

- Cardboard tubes, like from toilet paper or paper towels

- Egg cartons

- Paper bags

What you can do:

Use your imagination to combine your materials in cool ways. Here are some ideas to get you started.

- Tape tubes together to form a maze for the hamster to crawl through. You can sprinkle a few nuts or seeds in the maze to reward your hamster for going through.

- Glue a few boxes on top of each other to make a small tower. Your hamster will like climbing on it.

- Fasten tubes to a cardboard box so there are lots of little spaces for old Hammy to travel through to get in and out of the box.

- Place some shredded paper in an empty box or egg carton, and pretty soon, your hamster might nest down in it, cozy as can be.

Who knows? You might not even have a hamster. Your CLASS might not even have a hamster. But you can still use all these things to make cool mazes and launchpads for your toy cars, so have fun!

A bored hamster, is a <u>NOISY</u> hamster.

AWESOME HAIR

CHARMING SMILE

Zeke Meeks

COOLEST THIRD GRADER YOU'LL EVER MEET!